The **One** and **Only**
Sparkella

CHANNING TATUM

Illustrated by KIM BARNES

Feiwel and Friends

New York

A FEIWEL AND FRIENDS BOOK
An imprint of Macmillan Publishing Group, LLC
120 Broadway, New York, NY 10271
mackids.com

Our books may be purchased in bulk for promotional, educational, or business use.
Please contact your local bookseller or the Macmillan Corporate and Premium Sales Department
at (800) 221-7945 ext. 5442 or by email at MacmillanSpecialMarkets@macmillan.com.

Library of Congress Control Number: 2020919589

Book design by Sharismar Rodriguez
Feiwel and Friends logo designed by Filomena Tuosto
Printed in China by RR Donnelley Asia Printing Solutions Ltd., Dongguan City, Guangdong Province
First edition, 2021
ISBN 978-1-250-75075-4 (hardcover)
10 9 8 7 6 5 4 3 2 1
ISBN 978-1-250-81494-4 (special edition)
10 9 8 7 6 5 4 3 2 1

This is for Everly, the most brilliant magical being that
I have ever known. You are my greatest teacher. My only wish
is for more time in this life to play in all of the magical realms
we have created. This is also for all dads that might have
a little girl . . . Wear whatever, dance however, and be as
magical as you can. Because I promise they will return the love.
—C. T.

It is my first day at a new school.
I am ready.

Glimmering
pencil case?
Check!

Glittery ribbons
in my hair?
Check!

Shimmering
backpack?
Check!

Even my shoes glisten.
I am NOT nervous. Because I **SPARKLE**.

And this capital-P Princess Sparkella is ready to shine!
Dad throws on a fuchsia boa, and we are off.

The sunlight plays on my shoes and bracelets—
I am a walking disco ball!

Dad notices the dancing lights, and both of us
break out some moves.

My new school looks very different from my old school.
My palms start to sweat and my heart rate goes up.

But I am NOT nervous. Because I SPARKLE.

I notice that no one else does.

Kids look at me, and the parents stare at Dad.

"You ready, Sparkella?" Dad asks.

Maybe I am a *little* nervous.

I guess Dad can tell, because he puts on his *I'm going to give you a pep talk* face.

And after a few *yes you are*s and *no I'm not*s, Dad looks at me with that prime-time look and whispers, "Tiny dance party?"

I smile and laugh at our private dance party that's so tiny it's just for us.

With that, Dad gives me a great big hug and says goodbye.
I walk into my new school ready to take on the world.

But the world doesn't
seem ready for me.

The teacher introduces me to the other kids. "Everyone, please welcome Ella," she says.

I give my biggest smile.

You can call me Sparkella.

Someone in the back giggles, and not in a nice way.

At recess, a boy shouts, "Gah! Your shoes are blinding me!" which I know is not possible.

At lunch, a girl eating a boring ol' cheese sandwich tells me that my peanut butter, jelly, banana, and sprinkles sandwich looks gross.

And during art class, my painting of a unicorn doesn't get the response I thought it would.

Did I **SPARKLE** too much?

After school, Dad picks me up. He's now wearing a watermelon tutu. Some of the kids point and laugh.

The next day, I try to be less sparkly.

I wear gray pants, and I use my dad's tan backpack.

I tell Dad to take off his mint-colored tutu.

I am nervous.
And I do NOT sparkle.

When Dad drops me off, he asks, "You feeling okay, Ella?"
I don't answer; I just keep walking straight into school.

I sit quietly
at my desk.

I stand in my
square at recess.

I eat a peanut butter
sandwich with no jelly,
jam, fruit, or sprinkles . . .
just peanut butter
and bread!

I draw something boring.

And even though no one laughs or points at me,
I feel even worse.

That night, after dinner, Dad comes to my room. I am not in the mood for one of his pep talks. But to my surprise, he says:

Ella, I had a hard day at work.

I have an idea.

Do you know what I think would make you feel better?

I dim the lights and switch on my disco ball,
giving him my best prime-time face.

He smiles and turns the music way up.

We shake.
We shimmy.

We twist.
We twirl.

Afterward, I can tell Dad could still use some advice.
"What do we do when we're not sure how things will be?"

Dad closes his eyes and puts his hand over his heart.
I put my hand on his.

And we both say, "Close my eyes and know that
everything I could need is already there inside of me."

Then I say . . .

"And one more thing—WE SPARKLE!"

Dad gives me a big grin. "Thanks, Ella. It's hard
to be yourself sometimes."

"Yeah," I say. "And sometimes all you can do is be
more you-ish."

The next morning, I decide to
take my own advice.
I sparkle more than I ever have!

And when I come downstairs, Dad is sparkling, too.

"Ready for school, Ella?" he asks.

"I sure am, Dad," I answer. "And it's Sparkella."

I am nervous. And I also sparkle.

When I sit down at my desk, I notice the girl next to me is wearing a sparkly headband.

"Your headband is super cool," I say.

She smiles big and bright, and says, "Thanks! I love your shoes."

I am feeling less nervous, so I say, "My name is Ella. Actually, it's Sparkella."

"I'm Tam," she says.

At recess, Tam and I dance in the lights created
by our outfits. Tam is a really good dancer.
Some other kids join us.

I lend some sunglasses to the boy who complained
about my shoes—he does a silly dance.

During lunch, I give half of my almond butter, jam, blueberry, and whipped cream sandwich to Tam. She lets me try some of her bánh mì. It's delicious!

In art class, we paint flowers. A couple of kids don't understand my painting, but that's the thing about art— not everyone gets it!

After school, Dad is waiting for me in a bedazzled jacket and matching crown—he looks fabulous.

Some of the other parents stare, and now I can tell that they wish they shimmered as much as he does.

I think about meeting Tam and dancing together and sharing sandwiches and painting with my heart. Dad's right—it feels good to be yourself. There's only one word to describe how good my day was . . .

It SPARKLED!

Dad laughs. "Well of course it did, my little glitter poop."
I laugh and say I am not a glitter poop.

Yes you are no I'm not yesyouarenoI'mno